The World is Yours

By Megan Roth

Illustrated by Alina Chau, Federica Frenna,
and Tara Nicole Whitaker

Random House 🏠 New York

Copyright © 2020 Disney Enterprises Inc. Published in the United States by Random House Children's Books,
a division of Penguin Random House LLC, 1745 Broadway, New York, NY 10019, and in Canada by Penguin Random House
Canada Limited, Toronto, in conjunction with Disney Enterprises, Inc. Random House
and the colophon are registered trademarks of Penguin Random House LLC.
rhcbooks.com
ISBN 978-0-7364-4080-6
MANUFACTURED IN CHINA
10 9 8 7 6 5 4 3 2 1

It all begins with *a dream.*

For **adventure**.

For a little magic.

For *honor.*

For *freedom.*

For *something more.*

It all begins with a dream...

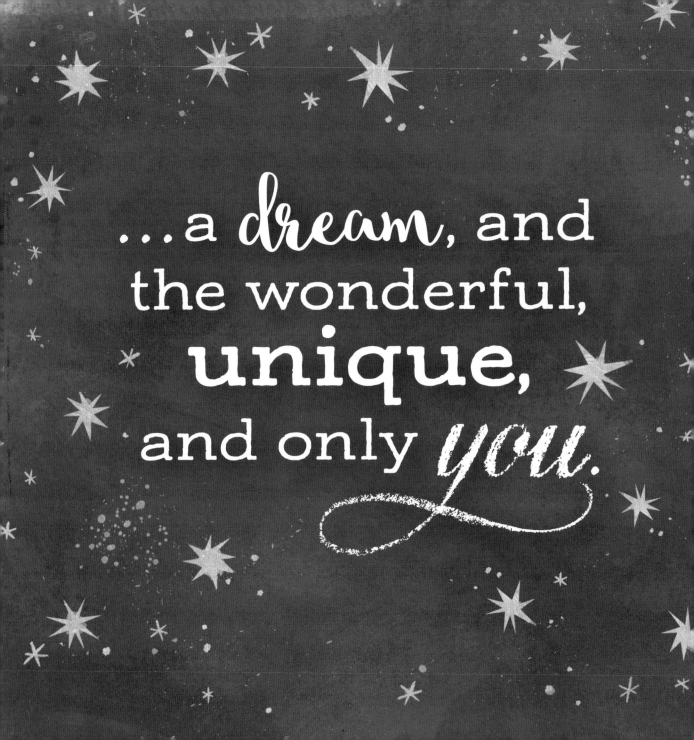
...a *dream*, and the wonderful, **unique,** and only *you.*

You're creative and
passionate.

You're not afraid
to embark on a
new journey.

You *never* give up
along the way.

You're *curious*
and *determined*.

You don't even need a *magic carpet*

Or a *genie's lamp.*

(Of course, they couldn't hurt.)

You already have EVERYTHING you need to make your *dreams* come true.

Because you have *you.*

The world is yours.
So dream your
biggest dreams... and
then dream even

BIGGER!